Virtual Heaven

Callum Davies

Copyright © Callum Davies 2024

All rights reserved. No part of this book may be reproduced or transmitted by any means, except as permitted by UK copyright law or the author. For licensing requests, please contact the author at callumdaviesauthor@gmx.co.uk

I dedicate this book to Marla, my whole world.
I also dedicate it to Russell for whom I am forever grateful to.
And finally I dedicate this book to my parents for their unwavering support.

Chapter One
Goodbye Faye

He sat beside her on the bed, holding on tightly to her cold hand. The room was illuminated with a dramatic, red glow by the neon sign displaying the words "Red Talon" outside the window, hanging above the entrance of their local bar. The sky was black. Beneath his feet, he could feel the slight vibration and hear the distant rattling of a nearby tram making its rounds through the bleak, gritty streets of the Forgotten.

His teary eyes were fixed upon her face, memorizing every single detail. She too looked upon him with unwavering love.

"I have this," Faye said in a soft, weakened voice as she slowly raised her right hand and retrieved something laying on the table beside the bed. It was a small, cylindrical device that resembled a cigar. She handed it to him.

"What is it?" he asked, curiously.

"It's called a Cortex," she explained as he examined it. "I took it from a Blue a month ago. Supposedly it stores your consciousness."

"How?" Jac asked, having never seen such a device before.

"The Blue said you're to place it against a person's head, right here," she continued, gesturing to the exact part of her head that she was referencing.

"It seems you had a nice chat with a Blue then," Jac smirked, and Faye did too. "Believe me, it wasn't by his choice." There was a brief moment of silence.

"I want you to do it when I die," she said. Jac, still holding onto her hand, caressing it with his thumb, looked at the Cortex once more, lost for words. "I don't want you to go," he pleaded, tears spilling. Faye placed her hand on his, and her touch was like ice.

"I'll die... but I wont be gone," she reassured him. "I will always be here."

"I love you Faye," Jac said, something he had said many, many times before, as he leaned in and kissed her lips.

"I love you too," she replied quietly, as their lips parted. "Goodbye Jac," she said, finally, in a whisper.

"Goodbye Faye," he replied as she slowly closed her beautiful green eyes. He exhaled suddenly, as though he had been holding his breath. He leaned forward and placed the device against Faye's head, like she had instructed. There was a faint whistling sound and then it stopped, replaced by a glowing, white light. Assuming it had worked, Jac moved the device away, placed it down and hugged her. Her frozen cheek pressed against his, and he was still holding on tightly to her hand. "I love you," he muttered under his breath.

A few months later...

"Jac!" a familiar voice called out. Jac, who was sat on his bed, was looking at the Cortex containing Faye's consciousness and he reminded himself, 'Not gone.' He turned around to see Maddox standing in the bedroom doorway. He had let himself in, as always. It had been a couple of weeks since they'd last seen each other. Although they weren't related, Maddox was like a brother to him. They had known each other since they were young. Maddox was slightly taller than Jac, and he was equally muscular with brown hair in a faux hawk style and a short beard. From the neck down, he was covered in tattoos.

"How's it going Mad Man?" Jac said, sliding the Cortex into the inner pocket of his long, leather overcoat. Despite his name being Maddox, Jac sometimes referred to him as Mad Man, a fitting alternative. Maddox was slightly unhinged, a result of both of Maddox's parents being killed by the Blues. The Blues was one of the nicknames given to the police because of their navy-blue gear. Maddox had also witnessed his brother being burned alive during their days in the underground.

There was no one that Jac knew who hated the Blues more than Maddox.

"I'm good man, how are you?" He asked as he and Jac exchanged a brief hug.

"I'm good," Jac replied. A lie that Maddox saw through. He still missed Faye. For anyone that knew Jac, they knew that Faye was his whole world. When she had died, a part of him had died too.

"What're you up to?" Jac asked. "I came to talk to you about something," Maddox replied, slightly lowering his voice.

"What is it?" Jac raised an eyebrow.

"We're planning on hitting a supply train tonight, coming from a supply station on the Welsh border," Maddox explained.

"The Welsh border?" Jack repeated, trying to make sense of it.

"We got some intel last night from someone who used to work on the supply train. He said that the supply train gets some of its supplies at the Welsh border, then it goes to Eden… join us," Maddox said.

"Where are the supplies from?" Jac wondered.

"No idea," he shrugged.

"Is this intel reliable?" Jac pondered.

"Yeah, the guy's in his late 50s. Apparently he stole some meds for his wife so they fired him. His wife died, he got upset and tried to make problems, so they banished him," Maddox went on. "He's living in the Forgotten now."

Jac thought about this for a moment while Maddox stood awaiting his response. "He says the last section of the supply train will be full of medicine, and we need it for the sick," Maddox said, in an attempt to persuade him to join. Jac's mind lingered on the word 'sick', and he immediately thought of Faye. With Faye gone, he had nothing to lose. Besides, medicine could help other women like Faye who were suffering from the same sickness.

They called it 'the Sleeper's Disease' as the only symptoms were severe weakness and fatigue. It was a disease that only affected women, and no one knew why. Due to the lack of medicine, it mostly ended in death. Although the Sleeper's Disease seemed to be passing, there were a lot of women still sick.

"Okay," Jac agreed with a look of determination upon his face.

"Good," Maddox said, placing a hand on his shoulder. "We're meeting tonight at the supply station on the Welsh border, near Raglan, at **4:30AM**."

"**4:30AM**? So tomorrow morning, not tonight?" Jac corrected.

"You know what I mean," Maddox replied, shrugging.

While thinking of Faye, Jac had forgot to ask something important. "How are we getting on the train?" he said.

"Seren has it planned, we should go and speak to her," Maddox said. "She's at the Red Talon."

Jac agreed. "Okay, let's go."

The two of them stepped out of Jac's apartment building onto the uneven pavement of one of the many miserable streets of the Forgotten. The name "Forgotten" was self explanatory. The Forgotten was the name of the South region of Wales. Only the people who couldn't afford to stay in Eden were there. While Eden thrived, the Forgotten and the rest of Wales did not. It was the same for Scotland too.

It was roughly **1:00PM** when Jac and Maddox made their way across the street to the bar opposite. Due to the dense smog that had swallowed the sky, it always looked as though it were the evening. The smog, mostly referred to as the 'choke smoke,' had been a consistent occurrence for the last forty four years. It was a result of mankind's neglecting of planet Earth. During those forty-four years of darkened sky, the suicide rate had escalated and still continued to. The smog had also brought forth a period called the Big Death that had seen the demise of a lot of animal life. Many people had never seen a blue sky, Jac and Maddox included. The lack of sunlight had resulted in everyone having a vitamin D deficiency as most people seemed pale faced, resembling ghosts. There were some places in the Forgotten that provided people with UVA light but it was costly.

Many people wore face masks to prevent themselves from breathing in the choke smoke but others, like Jac and Maddox, did not. In the Forgotten, if you didn't die as a result of breathing in too much choke smoke, sickness or starvation, you were at risk of being murdered by gangs and other deranged, bad people. The streets of the Forgotten weren't safe to walk, day or night.

There was Little Dublin, an area of Irish smugglers led by Hugh O'Shea, then there were the Welsh Insurgents, identifiable by the small symbol of two, red dragon wings on their clothing or tattooed on their upper arm. 'For Wales, we fight' was their motto, usually written in Welsh. They were for the people, and were a group who opposed the Blues and Eden itself. Then there was the worst of the worst, the Lurkers. They had gained their name by lurking in the shadows. They held no regard for human life, and were thieves, rapists, junkies, and murderers. It wasn't all criminals though. The Forgotten was also home to many unfortunate, normal people. Men, women and children trying to get by and survive in their unforgiving surroundings.

As Jac and Maddox entered the Red Talon, Jac immediately caught sight of Seren sat at the bar along with Celyn, Maddox's girlfriend. As they approached, Riley emerged from the bathroom, doing up his zipper.

"Aye! Aye!" Riley shouted across as he spotted them, getting Seren and Celyn's attention as they looked to him and then to the entrance where Jac and Maddox were.

Seren stood and greeted Jac with a welcoming hug. They were not only Jac's friends, he had once been their leader. He had run a small crew and together they had been responsible for numerous robberies against the Blues, stealing anything that would better the people of the Forgotten. Seren was Faye's best friend, and she was like a sister to Jac. They were both blonde and there was something of a resemblance between them. Celyn remained seated but said hello. She smiled as Maddox wrapped his arms around her from behind and smooched her head. Jac hadn't seen them in a while.

"How are you doing?" Jac asked Seren.

"You know, same shit different day," she replied, as they separated. He and Riley shook hands.

"How's it going lad?" Riley asked with his thick, Scottish accent. He was from the highlands.

"I'm alright like," Jac said, holding up his lie. Riley had reddish-brown hair, faded on the sides. Like Jac, he was clean shaven.

"Can I get you a drink?" Seren asked, as the barman stood awaiting their order. "I'll take a beer," Jac confirmed. As Riley walked away, he went and sat on a stool to Seren's left.

"Two beers," she said. Due to the lack of everything, she didn't need to specify what beer as there was only one brand of beer in the Forgotten, made locally in mid-Wales somewhere. She turned towards Jac. "So you agreed to come?" she said, with a slight smile.

"I did, but how do we get onto the supply train?" he asked, immediately getting to the point.

"Well, they don't expect anyone to try to get onto the supply train but we'll get on as it's leaving the supply station on the Welsh border," she explained, as the barman slid two bottles of slightly cold beer between them.

Both Seren and Jac picked up their beers and took a swig.

"Where are the supplies coming from?" Jac asked her.

"I have no idea," she admitted.

"How do we get onto the train?" He asked. There was a dense, bulletproof glass half-tunnel that the supply train went through, going all the way to Eden. The whole tunnel was lit up by lights and there were motion-detecting sentry turrets placed every 160ft. That was mainly the reason why they never expected anyone to try and get onto the train.

"There's a part of the tunnel where the lights are under repair, at the Welsh border. That's where we'll enter," she said.

"What about the motion-detecting sentry turrets?" He added.

"Maddox acquired some blackout cloaks from one of his contacts in the Welsh Insurgents," she replied.

Blackout cloaks prevented the wearer from being detectable by motion-detectors. "The back of the supply train is the least protected, so that's where we'd get on. We'll have a short window, maybe three seconds to jump onboard," she continued.

"Three seconds?" he said, looking unsure.

"Yes, three seconds," Seren confirmed.

"Will they hear us?" he asked.

"No, the exterior of the supply train is extremely thick," she said.

"And how do we get in?" he inquired further.

"With this," Seren said, holding up a keycard.

Jac seemed impressed. "How did you get that?" he asked.

"Didn't Maddox tell you?" She wondered.

"The guy in his 50s?" he remembered.

"Yeah, him. His name is Gareth."

Jac thought about it for a moment and asked, "If they fired him, wouldn't they have deactivated his keycard?" Seren smiled.

"They did but this isn't his keycard, he stole it." It was clear to Jac that this 'Gareth' had planned on having someone steal from the supply train from the beginning.

"I see... and how do we get off?" Jac concluded

"On the way to Eden, it passes through Bristol so we'll jump off there. Celyn's cousin has a boat, he'll take us across the River Severn."

"I see," Jac said, his mind void of any remaining questions. He took another swig of his beer. Jac was usually the one planning robberies, though they'd never planned anything THIS BIG. Though he had once been the leader of their crew, after Faye passed away, he had stepped back for a while. It appeared that Seren had taken the lead. He didn't mind though.

At that moment, two men entered the bar, one of who had a long, deep scar down the length of his face. They stared at Jac as they passed, and Jac stared back. One of them nudged into Seren as they moved to the bar. Maddox and Celyn were out back, and Riley was huddled over a jukebox as some mid-2000s music began playing.

"Oi, watch it!" Seren hissed. Jac stood.

"Shut up, you silly bitch!" the one man snarled. Jac stepped in front of Seren and punched the man in the side of the head. There was loud thud as his fist connected with the man's temple.

With a spray of spit, the man slumped onto the bar, knocking over his beer that the barman had just placed down, then he slid onto the floor. The other man, with the enormous scar, pulled out a big knife. "I'll fucking kill you!" he said through gritted teeth. Seren stayed put as Jac raised his fists.

"Come on then you prick!" Jac said. The man lunged forward. As he did, Riley hurdled over and punched him from behind. He went down, stiff, as though he were the statue of Edward Colston.

"Goodnight ya wee bastard," Riley muttered as the man hit the floor. Maddox and Celyn appeared from out back. "What happened?" Celyn said. "While you two were out getting some not so fresh air, me and Jac here were dealing with these two," Riley said, gesturing to the two men.

"Lurkers," Seren stated, downing the remainder of her beer, "I think that's our time to leave," she suggested.

As night fell, they all met up at the discussed location. It was **4:30AM** and in thirty minutes, the supply train would be departing from the Welsh border to reach Eden by **8:30AM**. There were two Blues stood near the entry point of the tunnel. Jac and the others had their ear pieces in and they were wearing the blackout cloaks with black half masks covering their mouths.

"Riley, you're up," Seren said as Riley then emerged from the shadows across from them, draped in a grey, tattered blanket. He scuffled towards the guards. "You! Stop there!" a Blue shouted, his gun aimed. The Blues moved towards him.

"I said stop!" one demanded.

"Now!" Seren said, as the rest of them emerged from behind the Blues. Jac and Maddox crept behind the unsuspecting guards, equipped with small knives.

With a signaling nod, they both immobilized the Blues permanently, and took their assault rifles and sidearms. Maddox slung his assault rifle over his back. Riley discarded the blanket as Jac threw him an assault rifle and he then hurried towards Seren and Celyn as Jac and Maddox dragged the lifeless guards away from preying eyes, behind some nearby debris. Moving silently, they regrouped with the others. Using the darkness to their advantage, they climbed up the half-tunnel using suction grips and prepared to jump onto the supply train. The huge doors of the supply station opened. Light from inside lit up the tracks as the front of the supply train was revealed, shaped like a 50cal bullet. The sound of the train's engine starting up sounded like a plane, a reference unknown to them. Then the train began to move, faster than Jac suspected.

"Ready yourselves," Seren said. "Ready… ready." They braced themselves and then suddenly, as the back of the supply train was passing, Seren shouted "Now!" The five of them leapt from the half-tunnel and onto the roof. No one fell. With that, they remained there for a moment as the immense doors to the supply station closed. They carefully climbed down onto the small platform at the back of the supply train where the back entrance was. Seren swiped the keycard and with a bleep, the door opened.

Chapter Two

River Severn

They entered the supply train. The interior of the supply train was like something Jac had never seen before. The lights were bright and the walls were white and silver. It was how Jac imagined the inside of a space shuttle looked; his dad had told him about one that a billionaire had launched once. This section of the train was full of stacked crates.

"We've hit the bloody jackpot!" laughed Riley as he pried opened one of the crates, revealing the neatly packed medication inside.

Seren smiled. "Okay, we don't have long. Take as much as you can," she said as everyone spread out.

Maddox opened a crate that appeared to be full of 500mg painkillers. He stuffed a few boxes into his satchel, while Celyn rummaged through a crate of vitamins, her eyes gleaming as though it contained golden coins.

After roughly twenty minutes, with everyone's bags full, there was a familiar bleep. The door from the other section opened and in stepped a guard. He was wearing a white shirt, a vest and slacks. Upon his head sat a peaked cap.

Everyone froze. Seren, who happened to be nearest to the door that the guard had come through, quickly swiped the keycard. With a bleep, the door sealed closed behind him. The guard spun around. Jac took the opportunity to pounce forward and apprehended the guard by grabbing him and pushing him against a crate. The guard's eyes widened as Jac pushed the tip of his handgun against the guard's throat, clasping a hand over his mouth.

"What should we do with him?" Celyn asked, with a look of concern. The guard's pleading was muffled by Jac's hand. Jac looked to Seren for an answer to Celyn's question.

While his head was turned, the guard grabbed Jac's hands and attempted to disarm him. Maddox aimed his assault rifle but couldn't get a clear shot.

"Don't shoot!" Celyn panicked. Jac and the guard struggled, grunting and shoving.

Seren was about to intervene when eventually Jac managed to angle the handgun downwards and fired. A bullet ripped through the guard's stomach. Celyn flinched. The thick walls of the supply train silenced the sound of the gunshot. The guard let go and groaned as he slumped to the ground, clenching his stomach.

"Okay, we need to go," Seren said, staying composed as she made her way to the back of the supply train.

"What about him?" Celyn asked, pointing to the bloodied guard at Jac's feet. Seren turned around. The guard reached into a pocket on his vest and took out a Cortex, which Jac recognized.

"Please, take this," the guard asked, holding the Cortex up.

"What is that?" Seren asked, moving closer.

"Please," the guard begged, before lowering his hand. Jac knelt beside the guard

"What does it do?" He asked.

Seren, ignoring the Cortex, turned back and said, "We need to go, now." She and the others headed to the back of the supply train.

"It takes your consci…"

"Yeah but then what?" Jac interrupted.

"You upload it to… Avalon," the guard said, his face draining, blood oozing from the bullet hole.

"What's Avalon?"

"Jac! We need to go, now!" Seren shouted, as she opened the supply train door.

"What is Avalon!" Jac insisted, clenching the man's shoulder.

"It's… it's a virtual he… heaven," the man muttered, releasing the Cortex from his grasp.

"Jac!" Seren called.

Jac had more questions than answers. A virtual heaven? The guard was bleeding out. Jac picked up the rolling Cortex and stood. He pointed the handgun at the guard's head and pulled the trigger. A bullet embedded itself in the guard's skull and blood sprayed, tarnishing the once plain white walls. Although Jac didn't have time to store the man's consciousness in his Cortex, he gave him a quick, painless death. Jac then hurried to the others and peered out into the darkness.

"Let's jump," Seren said as one by one they leapt from the train, landing onto the ground. The train sped on, disappearing into the distance, the sound fading.

Suddenly it was silent.

They clambered to their feet and ran to the side of the half-tunnel, undetectable to the sentry guns that surveyed the train tracks. They began to climb, using the suction grips once again. On the other side was Bristol.

"Celyn, which way?" Seren asked, once they were over.

"Follow me," she said confidently, as she lead them through Bristol. Bristol wasn't within the walls of Eden. It wasn't immaculate but it wasn't the Forgotten. The streets were clean and quiet, with no one around. They made their way to the dockyard at the waterfront.

"It's here," Celyn confirmed, pointing to a small boathouse. Upon entering, they were met by a man sat by a small table with scruffy hair. "Celyn!" He said, in a strong, Bristolian accent, jumping to his feet as they entered.

"How are you James?" she asked as the two of them hugged.

"How's it going James?" Maddox asked after with a nod.

"All good here," he replied, looking to the both of them.

"This is Seren," Celyn introduced.

"It's nice to meet you," James said, offering out a hand.

"Likewise," Seren said, accepting his handshake.

"Come on, lets go," James said as he ushered, wasting no time as he climbed onto the boat that was bobbing slightly on the water. As Jac climbed on, he was many miles away, still thinking of what the guard had said about Avalon and a virtual heaven.

The boat departed from Bristol and set off across the River Severn. When no one was looking, Jac felt into his pocket and took out the two Cortexes to get a quick glance. A white light was still glowing on one of them.

"Jac," Maddox said, getting his attention as he returned the Cortexes to his pocket.

"Yeah?" He said, facing him.

"You alright?" he asked, sitting beside him.

"Of course, that's not the first man I've killed," Jac reminded him. Both Jac and Maddox had killed their fair share of men, Blues and Lurkers.

"It's not that," Maddox hesitated, "You seem… distant."

"I'm fine," Jac lied. Yet another that Maddox could see through.

"I'm always here if you want to talk, you know that," Maddox assured him, unwilling to pressure him.

"I know," Jac confirmed, curling the corner of his mouth into a half- smile. Maddox nodded and returned to Celyn, putting an arm around her. She was talking to James.

"How's little Leo doing?" Celyn asked him. Leo was James's son. James chuckled, "He's not so little anymore, he's three now," he said, his eyes squinting, trying to see through the smog.

"Three! Already?" Celyn said in disbelief. "The last time I seen him he was still a little baby," she went on.

"I know, now he's walking and everything," he chuckled. "Wont be long and he'll be sailing my boat."

Because of the heavy smog, you could hardly see the water, although you could hear it splashing against the side of the boat. All around them was grey, and it was as though they were floating in an endless abyss. Jac could tell, somewhere, that the sun was rising because the sky was becoming a slightly lighter shade. They pushed through. Up ahead was the shore, appearing as a blackened silhouette.

"We're almost there," James announced, steering the boat inland. Soon, the boat rubbed against the soggy side of the wooden docks. James got off first and offered a hand to Celyn.

"Give my love to little Leo," Celyn said as she gave James a final, parting hug. "I will do," James agreed.

"Take care," said Maddox.

"Thank you for this" Seren said, shaking James's hand.

"No problem at all," James smiled. As they walked away, he jumped back onto his boat and set off back towards Bristol, the smog consuming him like a hungry monster.

Once they had reached the Forgotten, they took a few trams and, after walking for a while, they arrived at the Sanctuary to stash the bags and their equipment. The Sanctuary was their secret hideout in the Forgotten. It was in an old church. The inside of the church had mostly been renovated to have a lounge area, a kitchen, an armory, a gym, a bathroom and more. Seren approached Jac.

"Tomorrow me and the others will hand out the medication to anyone who needs it. You could help us," she suggested. Jac was still thinking about Avalon. He needed to know more.

"You guys got this," he said, a way of saying "No." Seren nodded. "Okay, well, see you soon," she concluded as she joined the others in inspecting their takings. "Well, see you guys," Jac waved as he was going. "Night lad!" Riley called after him.

Chapter Three

Avalon

Once again, Jac walked through the derelict streets of the Forgotten. He was headed to a place known as the Den, a hangout for tech-heads, gamers and hackers. If there was anyone who knew about Avalon, they'd be there. He passed a beggar, a decrepit man holding out a wireless card machine. "Could you spare me some bits?" He croaked. Physical money was long gone. The once 'Great British Pound' wasn't so great. It was all digital currency now. If you didn't have a card, you had nothing. The new currency was called 'Bits.' Jac took out his card and swiped it against the beggar's card machine. There was a 'ting' noise, confirming the transaction. "Thank you, thank you," the beggar said, cradling the card machine.

The GBP wasn't the only thing that had gone. So had the monarchy, abolished.

The United Kingdom was also no longer united. Wales, Scotland, and England were now all independent countries. Northern Ireland had joined the rest of Ireland back in 2026, a few years before the smog appeared and the world was overshadowed, although only Eden was plentiful. Jac knew little about Jonathan Eden or Eden itself. After the abolishment of the monarchy, also in 2026, Jonathan Eden became a dictator. Once the union had ended, Jonathan Eden renamed London 'Eden', after himself. He then began building the walls. The walls were 300m tall and had taken ten years to build. They encased the whole of Eden. It had cost billions, although no one knew from where Jonathan Eden had accumulated such wealth. Some say it was from the monarchy itself. Somehow Jonathan Eden had known what was coming. He allowed Wales, Scotland, and Ireland to remain unaware. All of Britain and beyond was covered in smog, tarnishing the once green grass as flowers withered away and many trees perished.

As well as Eden, Jonathan had put together an army. They were called the EDP (Eden Defense Personnel) but everyone referred to them as the Whites. Once the smog came, Eden was an indication of Jonathan's knowledge of it and so began the war, known as 'the Great Defeat.' Both Wales and Scotland joined together and attempted to attack England, specifically Eden, but they were defeated.

Because of Jonathan Eden, Eden's resources provided the EDP with more weapons and supplies. The Prime Minister of Scotland signed an agreement that Scotland would submit to England. The Prime Minister of Wales went into hiding with the help of the Welsh Insurgents. There was a long search for him but to no avail. There was some speculation that he had fled to Ireland but it wasn't confirmed, and the Irish government denied harboring him. Another man stepped up as the Prime Minister for Wales but he was disliked by all. He cared not for Wales. He was in Jonathan Eden's pocket. After the war, while Wales and Scotland were still diminished, Jonathan Eden deployed the Blues in both countries to make sure nothing like that happened again. Although Wales and Scotland remained independent countries, in a way, they were under the thumb of Jonathan Eden. Jac's father had fought in that very war and survived and until his death, Jac recalled him saying that one day, they'd fight again.

Religion had also disappeared. Everyone abandoned their churches, stopped believing in Jesus Christ and God and instead worshiped Bits or, in England, Jonathan Eden.

Jac arrived at a tram stop, which was full of people waiting. Shortly after arriving, the tram came. It wasn't manually driven, programmed with a specific route through the city. No ticket needed, you just got on. However, normally the tram was full. If so, people would climb onto the roof, as Jac did once the tram bumbled into the stop. The tram was rundown and completely covered in spray paint. The most noticeable was 'Fuck Tha Blues!' sprayed across the tram's doors. There was also a pair of red dragon wings, the sign of the Welsh Insurgents, a common graffiti found in the Forgotten. Jac climbed the tram and sat upon the roof for roughly fifteen minutes with his legs dangling off of the side as it rattled along before jumping off. Then, after a short walk, he was at the Den, a big building with a cyan neon sign angled slightly above the door. Jac could hear the muffled music from within. At the door stood a tall, brawny man, almost as wide as the doorway. He was bald and had tattoos all over his face. There was an array of CCTV cameras displayed above him.

"Biscuit," Jac said as he approached the bouncer. Biscuit wasn't a password. It was the bouncer's nickname. He had earned the nickname because he was tough, the opposite of a biscuit.

"Jac," Biscuit greeted, in a deep voice, stepping aside. Jac was known in the Den. He headed down a dimly lit corridor and into a huge room. The inside of the Den was full of computers with at least one person sat in front of each of them, lit up by the screens. Either gaming, hacking or some other tech-related stuff that Jac didn't understand. In one corner were a bunch of people standing, wearing VR goggles. It made sense to Jac that people would rather remain in a virtual reality as apposed to their own, especially here in the Forgotten. It was loud in the Den. There were speakers set up in the corners of the room playing EDM music. The walls and floor were grubby. After all, it had once been an abandoned warehouse. There were thousands of cables hanging from the ceiling and sprawled across the floor.

"Do you know of Avalon?" Jac asked a young, slim man, staring at his screen. He was playing an RPG game, which was reflected in his eyes.

"No idea what that is," the young man replied in a nasally voice without even looking up. Jac moved on and asked another.

"Do you now anything about Avalon?" He questioned. This kid was wearing a headset.

"What the fuck are you doing!?" the kid huffed to whoever was on headset with him. He was oblivious to Jac's presence and question. Jac sighed and moved on. He went up the stairs to an area full of people who seemed less focused.

"Does anyone know anything about Avalon?" Jac asked a group of people gathered around a table. They shook their heads. Jac wasn't sure who to ask. As he glanced around, a different bouncer came up to him.

"Jac," the man said. Jac turned to face him.

"Yeah?" he answered.

"You want to know about Avalon?" the man asked. Jac was hesitant.

"I do," he replied.

"Follow me," the bouncer insisted as he led Jac down a hallway to a door with the word 'Private' on it. Jac entered a room with a similar décor to the rest of the Den. There was a desk with an impressive set up of three monitors on it. Behind the monitors sat a spectacle-wearing kid in his late teens, slumped in an armchair.

The bouncer closed the door behind Jac.

"Hello," the kid said.

"Hello," Jac said back.

"My names Rhys," the kid introduced himself.

"My names J.."

"Jac," Rhys interrupted, "I know," he admitted. Jac looked confused.

"I know everyone who comes to the Den, I was watching you on the cameras... see." Rhys said, pointing to one of the three monitors. Jac went around Rhys's desk and looked. Rhys appeared to have access to all of the security cameras.

"Who are you?" Jac asked. He'd been to the Den many times and had never seen Rhys there before.

"I'm Rhys," he said again, "I'm in charge."

"You are in charge?" Jac asked.

"Yes," Rhys confirmed. "I heard you asking about Avalon," he continued.

"I was," Jac said quickly, moving on. "Do you know of it?" he inquired.

"I do... very well," Rhys admitted. Rhys pressed a few keys on his keyboard and pointed at his monitor again. Jac took a look.

On the screen was a picture of a huge, white machine.

"That's Avalon," Rhys confirmed. Jac looked at it for a moment. "What did you want to know?"

"I've heard it's a virtual heaven?" Jac said, finally looking back at Rhys.

"It is," Rhys confirmed, as though it were common knowledge. "In Eden, using a device called a Cortex, you upload the consciousness of the deceased to Avalon, a virtual heaven. Once their consciousness has been uploaded, the deceased live again, virtually, in a heaven constructed of their best memories," Rhys rambled on.

"A Cortex," Jac remembered. He took Faye's Cortex from his inner pocket. "This.." He showed it to Rhys. Rhys's eyes lit up.

"Yes!" He said, excitedly. "I've never seen one in person before. Can I take a look?" Rhys asked, reaching out.

Jac pulled the Cortex away. Rhys noticed the glowing white light on the Cortex. His look of excitement faded. "It contains someone's consciousness," Rhys stated. Jac nodded.

"Yes, my wife," he confessed.

"I'm sorry," Rhys sighed. "Well... as I said, Avalon is in Eden I'm afraid…" Rhys went on.

"I know," Jac replied, swapping Faye's Cortex for the other one. "There's something else," Jac confessed, handing Rhys the empty one. Rhys took it and analyzed it, twisting it and turning it.

"What is it?" Rhys asked. "I want to store my consciousness to that one," he said. Rhys looked up, "If you do that, the physical you will die," Rhys explained. "I know," Jac said. "I want to upload my consciousness, and that of my wife, to Avalon at the same time. Is there a way?" Jac inquired. Rhys, ignoring the sadness of the question, thought about it for a moment and then his eyes lit up once more.

"Yes… yes there is," Rhys said, looking pleased. Jac also looked the same.

"How?" Jac asked.

"If I can combine these two Cortexes so then they share the same transmitter, then there is a way," Rhys said, walking to a bench containing a heap of parts.

"But storing my consciousness will kill me, right?" Jac said.

"It will but if I can add this to the empty one, you can upload the two Cortexes and then store your consciousness," Rhys revealed, holding up what seemed to be black lead.

Jac stood by watching as Rhys rummaged through the parts occasionally mumbling "Yes," or "Hmm." Rhys had removed the part from the empty Cortex that was placed against the head and instead attached it to the black lead.

Then he attached the two Cortexes together. Rhys took off his glasses and slipped on a pair of goggles. There were a few sparks and flashes of light as he used a laser to weld them together. The whole process took roughly ten minutes. Rhys flung the goggles off, slid his glasses back on, spun around and presented Jac with the finished piece. He looked at it. He was relieved that the glowing, white light of Faye's Cortex was still there, intact.

"So, what you will need to do is insert this into Avalon. You then need to place this lead against your head right here," Rhys gestured.

"Yeah I know," Jac dismissed, taking the Cortexes. "And it will work?"

"It will," he insisted. He looked both pleased with his handiwork and disheartened that Jac intended on ending his seemingly healthy life. "How many bits?" Jac asked as he returned the Cortexes to the confines of his inner pocket.

"Nothing," Rhys said, a display of kindness. "But as I said, Avalon is in Eden, there's no way you'll get in," he reminded Jac.

"I'll find a way," Jac said as he walked towards the door. Before leaving, he turned once more.

"Thanks kid," he said as he left.

The bouncer was stood outside the door. He followed Jac back down the hallway and then dispersed. Jac made his way back down the steps, pushing through the crowds of people, most of them wearing VR goggles. He then exited the Den and bid farewell to Biscuit, who was stood so still that it was as though he was a statue.

Jac returned to his apartment and sat down in an armchair. He took out the Cortexes and examined them once again before placing them on a table. He began to think about how he would get into Eden. If there was anyone that could get him in, it was Hugh O'Shea. Jac knew it would be costly but he had 30,000 bits on his card. He had accumulated them from various robberies. The view outside of Jac's apartment looked like an apocalypse. Occasionally, the odd shadowy figure darted through the street and down some narrow alleyway.

Jac went to the kitchen and took a beer from the fridge. There were three remaining beside a feeble assortment of food. He fell back into the armchair and put his feet up on the table. He swiped up the TV remote beside him and turned on the TV. It was a 77", 4k, high resolution, curved screen TV. Very basic for its time. He clicked aimlessly through the channels. Despite it being late, the Forgotten never slept. He could hear distant shouting and something smashing from time to time. The closer you were to the walls of Eden, the more presence of the Blues you'd see but here, in the depths of the Forgotten, it was basically lawless and unhinged, apart from the occasional patrol but that was never at night. Nighttime belonged to the Lurkers.

There wasn't much to watch on TV; the news was shit and biased, and there were no new movies or shows, just old reruns. A lot of the channels were full of counter propaganda being shown by the Welsh Insurgents. They were constantly hacking the broadcasting station. Jac put down the remote, twisted off the bottle top and started sipping his beer. He didn't like being in this apartment, not since Faye had passed away. It felt empty. The very person that had made the apartment home was now no more than a glowing white light on a device. It felt cold, not just the apartment and the Forgotten but life itself. Jac kept his eyes on the TV. He couldn't bare to see the framed pictures of him and Faye, even though he didn't have the heart to put them away. His moment of quietness came to an end with a knock on the door.

It wasn't Maddox. He always let himself in. It was too firm to be Celyn and Seren always kicked it instead of knocking. No idea why. Jac remained seated for a moment, ignoring it, assuming it was just his neighbor. He was usually drunk, fumbling around trying to get into his apartment. But then there was another knock. Jac got to his feet, put down the beer and strolled to the door. Peering through the peephole would be useless as the lights on the stairwell didn't work. He pulled open the door and there stood before him in the darkness was Riley.

"Hello lad," Riley said.

"Riley," Jac replied, unsure of why he was here.

"You gonna let me in or am I to stand out here in the dark?" He smirked.

Jac moved aside as Riley then entered the apartment. Jac closed the door behind him.

"Is everything alright?" Jac asked as he quickly moved the Cortexes from the table and put them in a drawer.

"Aye, swell," Riley muttered as he glanced around. Jac flicked the switch on a lamp, adding some life to the room.

"What brings you here then?" Jac wondered, heading to his kitchen to get Riley a beer.

"I'm going back to Scotland," Riley said as he sat himself down on the sofa. Jac came back into the living room and handed him the beer. "Ah, thank you." He took a gulp.

"How come?" Jac asked him as he sat down near him.

"Well… I miss Scotland, though it's not much different than here, it's home, ya know?" he went on. Jac sat listening. "Plus, my wee sister has just had a bairn too," he said, smiling.

"Congrats, that's great," Jac grinned.

"Aye," Riley nodded.

"Girl or boy?" Jac asked him.

"A wee boy, look, my sister sent me this," Riley said as he took out a photograph from his pocket and held it up for Jac to see. There was a woman, presumably Riley's sister holding a baby.

"What have they named him?" he asked. Riley put the photo away.

"Alexander," he said. "So in a couple of days I'll be boarding a passenger train to Scotland," he explained. The passenger trains were difficult to get on. They travelled from Wales, through England and up to Scotland. They were always guarded by the Blues. You needed proper passes to get on one. The real passes were incredibly difficult to get but Riley had used the money from a robbery a few weeks back to get himself a counterfeit.

"Well, I'm happy for you, uncle Riley," Jac laughed as he raised his beer.

Riley did too.

"Well, if you're going, I think we should get hammered," Jac shrugged.

"Aye… I think so."

Chapter Four

The Blues

It was the morning, Jac opened his eyes and with slightly blurred vision, he looked around. There were a number of empty beer bottles on the table. To his left, sprawled out, was Riley, snoring. There was a small thumping in Jac's head. He sat up and stretched before climbing to his feet. He shuffled to his bedroom to get himself some clean clothes, the usual black trousers and black tank top. Then he shuffled to the bathroom and locked the door behind him. He took off his underwear and stepped into the shower. After a quick wash, he stepped back out, dried himself off and got dressed. He did his hair in the mirror, slicking it back and then left. Riley was sat up rubbing his head.

"You're alive then," Jac said as he walked by.

"Ugh… ma heid," Riley groaned. Last night, after they drank the two remaining beers in the fridge, they decided to go to the Red Talon. They drank beer after beer after beer, and then Riley attempted to chat up a woman using his 'Scottish charm,' as he called it, which had resulted in him getting smacked across the face. Afterwards, he had kept saying how he was "deeply in love." They were at the bar until **3:00AM** until they finally went back to the apartment, taking a few beers with them. Then at **5:00AM,** they stopped drinking and passed out on the sofa.

"It feels like someone's been tap dancing on ma heid," he moaned. As he got up. Jac laughed as he peered into his fridge. "Ah shite," Riley huffed.

Jac swung the fridge door closed.

"What?" he asked.

"I forgot I got a tattoo appointment today," he said in a moment of sudden remembrance.

"Where?" Jac wondered.

"Lucky 7, do you know it?" Riley asked.

"Yeah I do," Jac confirmed. Lucky 7 was a tattoo shop not too far from Jac's apartment. It was where he and Faye had gone to get their tattoos. It was also where a lot of the Welsh Insurgents went to get their tattoos of recognition.

"My appointment is in an hour," he said, having glanced at the digital clock on the wall.

"Well, the fridge is empty so I say we get some brekkie on the way," Jac suggested.

"Aye," Riley agreed as Jac slid on his boots and put on his leather overcoat, leaving the Cortexes behind. They took the elevator down from the fifth floor and passed an elderly man with a synthetic ear, a replacement of the outdated hearing aid. On their way to the tattoo studio, they stopped by a small food stand with a holographic sign saying, 'Jon's Baps.'

"Hello Jon," Jac said as he arrived. Jon was grilling up some bacon. He looked over his shoulder at them.

"Ah, hello boyo!" Jon beamed "It's been a while," he said. Jon was a short, plump man in his fifties with some hair clinging on desperately to his head. He had been running this food stand for years. He had been running it with his son, Liam, until he had joined the Welsh Insurgents and got himself killed. Other than the stand, Jon had nothing. In fact, he lived in the stand. Although the Forgotten was a bad place, everyone respected Jon.

"I know, yeah," Jac agreed. "This is Riley," he introduced.

"Ello mate." Riley said offering out a hand. Jon wiped his greasy hands into his apron and shook it.

"Nice to meet you, is that a Scottish accent I detect?" Jon asked.

"Aye, it is indeed," Riley confirmed.

"What can I get you boys?" Jon asked as he leaned on the front counter. Jac stared at the menu on the screen beside him. It showed a few different baps with their names.

"I'll have a bacon and egg bap," Jac decided, Jon nodded approvingly.

"Aye, same for me too," Riley said.

"Rightyo!" Jon said as he turned around and returned to the grill. Jac swiped his card against the card machine and heard the familiar 'ting.'

"Brekkie is on me," Jac winked.

"If I didn't know any better, I'd say this was a date," Riley joked as they took a seat at a table set up by the food stand. The smell of the sizzling bacon lingered around them.

"So, what tattoo are you getting?" Jac asked. Riley lifted up his t-shirt, showing his stomach.

"I'm getting a tattoo of a claymore here," he pointed.

"A what?" Jac asked.

"A claymore. It was a sword used by Scottish highlanders," Riley explained.

"I see," Jac said, admiringly, as Riley adjusted his t-shirt.

"Your baps boys!" Jon called out not long after. They got up, grabbed their food, said their thanks and sat back down again. The two of them wasted no time in taking a bite.

"Mmmm," Riley mumbled as he swallowed. "That's braw," he admitted. Once the baps had been completely devoured, the two of them said their goodbyes to Jon and wished him well before continuing on their way, arriving shortly after at the tattoo studio.

Someone was leaving with a freshly wrapped tattoo as the two of them entered, and they were met with a big, towering man, covered from neck to ankles in tattoos.

Hanging from his face was a big, bushy beard of the fieriest ginger. This was the tattooist, Steve. Beside him stood his wife, Jan, who had a head of curly, blonde hair. She too was covered in tattoos. She was a body piercer.

"This way," Jan said to a woman waiting, as she led her into a different room. "Ello, I have an appointment for a tattoo," Riley said.

"Riley, yeah?" Steve asked, as he ran his finger down the open page of his appointment book.

"Aye," Riley confirmed. Steve closed the book.

"Take a seat while I set up," he said.

The two of them did. The walls of the studio were plastered with tattoo designs and other artwork and ornaments. As they were waiting, the loud, screeching noise of tires came from outside.

Jac turned his head to see a big navy vehicle, covered in armored plating, at the entrance. His eyes widened. Before he could say anything, the door to Lucky 7 burst open and in charged three Blues armed with assault rifles, followed by a sergeant.

"Nobody move!" One of the Blues shouted. Both Jac and Riley jumped to their feet. Steve stood still, holding his tattoo machine.

"Drop it!" one Blue shouted to Steve, as though he were holding a weapon, as the two other Blues aimed their guns at Jac and Riley. Steve complied.

"Put your hands up! Now!" Another bellowed. Jac noticed that there were two more Blues stood outside. The sergeant removed his helmet.

"I'm Sergeant Baker," he said, puffing out his chest. "We have reason to believe this place is used by the Welsh Insurgents," he said. His face was stern.

The door to the piercing room opened and out came the woman, yet to have had her piercing. "I'm just a client," she said, holding up her hands. The sergeant signaled her to leave with a flick of his head. As she walked past, he grabbed her arm.

"Oi!" she mouthed. The sergeant rolled up her sleeve, revealing a small tattoo of red dragon wings. The sergeant smiled malevolently.

"Take her," he ordered as one of the Blues grabbed her. She was squirming as he dragged her out of the tattoo studio.

"Get the fuck off me!" she spat. The sergeant, with his helmet tucked under his arm, walked up to Steve who still hadn't moved.

"It appears you are allowing members of the Welsh Insurgents onto your premises and providing them with their markings" The sergeant scolded. Steve's wife stood nearby. The sergeant looked to her and then back to Steve. "You two will be arrested for assisting terrorists and your studio will be terminated," He stated, before turning to Jac and Riley. "Check them for the wing tattoo" He ordered. As the two remaining Blues were about to do so, Riley spoke.

"You're awfully brave for a wee man," Riley mocked. Jac gave Riley a side glance, wishing he had remained silent.

"What?" the sergeant scowled.

'Shut up,' Jac thought to himself.

"I said… you are awfully brave for a wee man," Riley repeated.

'Fuck…' Jac thought. The sergeant looked visibly appalled by the disrespect. He unholstered his sidearm and without mercy, he unloaded multiple bullets into Riley.

"No!" Jac shouted. With a roar, Steve grabbed the sergeant from behind, lifted him and slammed him onto the ground, his head splitting, killing him. Jac front kicked one of the Blue's in the abdomen, hurling him back. Jac then grabbed the Blue's assault rifle, pressed the barrel against him and in a frenzy, squeezed the trigger, unleashing bullets that ripped through the Blue's chest. Blood sprayed. The last remaining Blue stood, disorientated. Jan grabbed a handgun concealed under the front desk, aimed, and pulled the trigger. One single golden bullet entered through the opening of the Blue's helmet and went through his head. Blood splattered. The Blue fell.

Jac turned to the entrance where three more Blues were hurrying towards him. He squeezed the trigger again. Bullets sprayed. The glass door disintegrated.

The woman took cover behind the Blue's vehicle as the three of them were littered with holes and they too died. The woman, along with other passerbys, fled. Jac dropped the assault rifle. Golden bullet casings were scattered all around him. He knelt beside Riley who was slumped on the floor. No final words, no snarky remarks, he was dead. "You and your big mouth," Jac mumbled as he closed Riley's empty, lifeless eyes.

"There's a back exit, we should go," Jan said. Jac took the photograph from Riley's pocket and followed them. They came out into an alleyway behind the tattoo shop. "We're sorry about you friend," Jan sympathized, and she and Steve headed down the alleyway and disappeared. Jac composed himself. Droplets of blood were speckled across his face like freckles. He took a deep breath and went a different direction than they did. He stayed away from main roads. Instead, he went through lanes and alleyways, blending in with the homeless and beggars that resided there, a few of them uttering "Please spare some bits," as he passed.

Finally he exited an alleyway and arrived at the Sanctuary. He entered and found Maddox and Celyn, who were talking. They both looked at Jac as he came in, and they could see the blood.

"What happened, brother?" Maddox asked, with a look of concern. Celyn gasped.

"Riley's dead," he said abruptly.

"Wha… what?" Maddox said, taken aback. Celyn clasped her hands over her mouth. Jac took a seat, grabbed a cloth, and began wiping his face.

"How? Wh… what happened?" Maddox asked, approaching him.

"We were at Lucky 7, Riley was getting a tattoo and then the Blues raided," Jac explained. Maddox knew Lucky 7 was a place frequented by the Welsh Insurgents, he had also gotten his tattoo there. "He… he just couldn't keep his mouth shut," Jac grunted, throwing the cloth down. "He… he insulted a sergeant… the sergeant killed him," he finished.

"What happened then?" Maddox inquired further, tensing up.

"We killed them," Jac revealed. He ran his hand through his hair. "He was supposed to be returning to Scotland," Jac said. "His sister had just given birth."

"Fuckers!" Maddox bellowed in a sudden outburst, flinging a chair across the room, startling Celyn.

"Are you okay?" she blubbered, looking at Jac with sorrowful eyes.

"I'm fine," Jac dismissed. For Maddox, it reignited his hatred for the Blues. What Jac didn't know was that Maddox and Riley had become really good friends during Jac's absence.

"Where is he now?" Maddox asked as Celyn caressed his arm to calm him.

"I left him," Jac said, "I couldn't take him with me." Maddox thought for a moment.

"They'd have taken him to the mortuary," he stated. "Me and Celyn will steal his body… we should bury him." Celyn nodded in agreement. Jac too. Jac stood up. "I have this," He said, showing them the photograph, now slightly crumpled. Jac handed it to Maddox.

"We should bury it with him," he insisted. Maddox took the photograph, looked at it and slid it away. For a moment, no one said anything.

"I'm going home," Jac sighed, Maddox patted his shoulder as he passed him. "Meet me here tomorrow morning," Maddox said, "We'll bury Riley then." Jac simply nodded and left.

Chapter Five

The Burial

Morning had arrived. Jac had barely slept. All night, he kept thinking of Riley, re-living it in his head. He had finally fallen asleep at **6:15AM** and was awake by **8:00AM**. As always, he got up, showered, got dressed and styled his hair. He wasn't hungry so he left his apartment without breakfast, not that his fridge held much option.

He set off towards the Sanctuary. On his way, he noticed an increased Blues presence. It must have been because of what had happened yesterday. Once he got to the Sanctuary, Seren was stood outside with a woman Jac had never seen. "Jac!" Seren said aloud, "Are you okay?" she asked, holding him. "Maddox told me what happened," she sighed.

"I'm good," he said.

"Maddox and Celyn brought his body to the Sanctuary," she told him.

"I know, he said they would," he said. Seren let go of him.

"This is Naja, my girlfriend," she introduced. Naja smiled. Jac hadn't known Seren was seeing someone. Naja was a short, dark skinned woman with black hair in two braids.

"Hey," she said.

"Hello," Jac said back.

"Come on, everything's ready," Seren notified, leading him in with Naja following alongside.

As they entered, laid upon what was once an altar for religious ceremonies, was Riley's body. He had a blanket draped over him with his shoes protruding from the bottom. On his chest was the photograph. Maddox and Celyn were stood nearby.

"How did it go?" Jac asked Maddox, and Maddox turned his head to reply. "All good, no problems," he assured. Naja pulled the Sanctuary doors closed. Jac approached the altar, looking down at Riley. He took a deep breath.

"He was often annoying and he never knew when to shut up," Jac started, "But... he was my friend, our friend. Riley always had our backs. The last thing he said was 'You're awfully brave for a wee man,' to a sergeant." The others laughed. "He'd have been happy knowing they were his last words," Jac declared. They all mumbled in agreement. "To Riley!" Jac yelled.

"To Riley!" the other's repeated.

"May the wind carry his soul to Scotland," he concluded, placing a hand on Riley's arm. Jac moved away, allowing someone else to say something. Maddox stepped up next.

Once everyone had said their piece, Jac and Maddox carried Riley out of the Sanctuary to the graveyard behind it. The women had cleared away the litter while Maddox had dug up someone from the 1800s to lay Riley there instead. After they had slowly lowered him into the ground, the two of them covered him over. Burials were unheard of now. The deceased were always incinerated.

After the smog, the Great Defeat and the Sleeper's Disease, there were too many bodies, so cremating the deceased was more convenient and became mandatory.

But Riley had always said he wanted to be buried. He would say 'I want to be buried like my great, great granda.' Once Riley was six feet beneath the decaying Earth, they met at their usual, the Red Talon, for Riley's wake, to drink in his honour and memory. They played his usual 2000s music and drank the same beer.

"What happened to the tattooist and his wife?" Maddox asked Jac.

"The two of them fled," Jac said as Seren, Naja and Celyn danced.

"I'm thinking of rejoining the Insurgents," Maddox confessed.

"Does Celyn know?" Jac asked him, doubtful she did.

"No," Maddox admitted. As Jac had thought. "With what happened to Riley and knowing the Insurgents are still going, it made me realise there was no great defeat. We lost the war, but we're still fighting," he ranted.

He had a point. Jac would have gone with Maddox but he had something else to do – to get into Eden. Knowing that he and Faye could meet again, even if it was virtually, was worth it. That meant more to him than joining the Welsh Insurgents, fighting the Blues, and restoring the Forgotten.

"What will Celyn say?" Jac asked.

"She'll understand. She knows how much the Blues have taken from me," he said. Soon after, once the music had stopped, everyone left the Red Talon and parted ways. Jac, who had only had one beer, returned once more to his apartment. He kicked off his boots, slouched onto his bed and nodded off.

Chapter Six

The Irish

The following morning, Jac took the Cortexes from the drawer and went to the Sanctuary. As he entered, Maddox and Celyn were discussing Maddox's intention of rejoining the Welsh Insurgents.

"They killed my parents, my brother, many of my friends, Riley included," Maddox explained to her.

Jac, remaining unnoticed, went and sat by Seren who was observing their discussion.

"I know and I understand, I do, but what if the Blues take you from me?" Celyn reasoned.

"Maddox wants to rejoin the Insurgents," Seren whispered to Jac.

"Yeah, I know," he whispered back. Jac wanted to tell them he was going to find a way into Eden but he knew they'd try to talk him out of it. So, instead, he planned on telling them that he was going to travel to Ireland for some time away. A partial truth. He would, after all, be going to Little Dublin to speak to Hugh O'Shea.

"They wont take me from you," Maddox assured her.

"You don't know," she argued. "If you want to rejoin the Insurgents, do it. But don't get yourself killed," she said.

"I wont," he told her as she embraced him.

Naja entered the Sanctuary, bringing refreshments. Her presence did not go unnoticed.

"Jac," Maddox said, upon seeing him sitting there.

"Alright?" Jac said. Naja went and sat on the other side of Seren.

"Hi babe," she greeted, kissing her, and passing her a drink.

With the Cortexes in Jac's inner pocket, he got to his feet. Now was the time. "Listen," he beckoned, as all eyes fell upon him. "I've decided I'm going to Ireland for a while, clear my mind," he announced. "I'm leaving today." They all looked surprised.

"How long for?" Seren asked.

"A few months," Jac lied.

"I'll miss you brother," Maddox admitted as he came towards him, arms wide. Jac indulged him and the two of them hugged.

"I think it will do you good," Maddox insisted.

"As Celyn said, don't go getting yourself killed," Jac told him.

"I wont, I wont," he dismissed.

"I know you'll look after him," Jac said to Celyn.

She smiled, "Always."

Jac turned to Seren. "You've done a good job running this crew," Jac said. "I'll leave knowing it's in good hands," he nodded. Seren smiled at him.

"It'll never be the same without you… or Faye," she responded.

"I know," he muttered. "Good luck putting up with her," he joked to Naja.

"Thank you," she giggled.

"Be well Jac," Seren said.

"Yeah, look after yourself brother. I'll be here," Maddox added.

"Take care guys," Jac said, knowing that whatever happened, he'd never see them again. He left the Sanctuary, pulling its doors closed behind him. He took one final look at the church and walked away.

He was going to Little Dublin. Little Dublin was a small area of Irish criminals and smugglers. Their leader, Hugh O'Shea, was who he was going to see. If there was anyone in the Forgotten that could get him beyond the walls and into Eden, it was him. As he walked through Little Dublin to the dockyard, where Hugh was, he was met by a tall muscular man leaning against a wall.

"Who are ye?" The man asked as he confronted Jac.

"My names Jac, I'm here to see Hugh O'Shea," he revealed. The Irishman stared down at him, as though he were trying to intimidate him. "He knows me," Jac insisted, unfazed.

"Follow me," the man muttered. He led Jac through the dockyard and into a warehouse. In the warehouse was an impressively large boat with 'Ériu' written on it, presumably the name of the ship. There were men unloading crates from it. The crates looked familiar. The big man led Jac up some stairs and into an office that overlooked the warehouse. Hugh O'Shea was sat with his feet upon a desk.

"Jac!" Hugh welcomed as he entered, surprised to see him.

"Hugh," Jac nodded. Hugh tipped the brim of his trilby.

"How's it going?" Hugh asked, "It's been a while?" The last time Jac had seen Hugh, he had helped them get some of Maddox's friends from the Welsh Insurgents, onto a boat to Ireland.

"What brings ye here?" he asked. Jac looked over his shoulder, the big Irishman that led him here loomed behind him. "Away with ye Bren, standing behind him like a bleeding wall," Hugh said to the man. Brennan left, closing the office door behind him. "Well?" Hugh said.

"I need to get into Eden," Jac stated.

"Eden you say?" Hugh seemed intrigued. "That'll cost ye lad," he admitted.

"I know… I'll pay you well," Jac bargained, placing his card on the desk and sliding it across to Hugh. Hugh picked it up and scanned it with a handheld device. By scanning it, the device told Hugh how many bits the card contained. "Thirty thousand bits!" Hugh exclaimed, reading it, his eyes glistening. "How did a man like yourself come into possession of so many?"

Hugh asked.

"Can you get me in?" Jac pressured, ignoring Hugh's question.

"Aye, for thirty thousand bits, I'll get you anywhere," He grinned.

"When?" Jac asked

"I can get you in tonight," Hugh revealed.

"Good," Jac nodded. Hugh stood, leant over his desk and the two of them shook hands.

"That's a deal then," Hugh smirked, tucking the card into his pocket.

"That's an impressive boat out there," Jac said.

"Aye, it is that, not long arrived from Ireland she has," he told him as he walked to the office window and watched as his men finished unloading.

"So. How do I get in?" Jac queried.

"Well, there's only one way you can get in to Eden," Hugh said.

"How?" Jac asked. Hugh walked up to Jac.

"The supply train," he answered.

"How do I get onto the supply train and remain unseen?" he questioned.

"I can smuggle you into a crate on the supply train. The crates are perforated, so you'll be able to breath," Hugh replied. At that moment, Jac realized that the crates Hugh's men were unloading were the same as the ones that they had plundered on the supply train. That meant that Hugh was one of the suppliers, meaning technically they'd robbed Hugh, not Eden. Hugh was playing a risky game, assisting the people of the Forgotten for bits and supplying Eden, no doubt for bits. A middle man. Eden must have been paying him handsomely. How else would he afford such a boat? "No one checks the crates, so you wont be found either," Hugh reassured him.

"I see," Jac said, as all of his thoughts swirled around his mind. Jac couldn't help himself. He needed to know more. "So, you supply Eden," he said.

"Aye, I know they're a bunch of bastards but they pay me well," Hugh shrugged. A lot of people were suffering because of Eden and Hugh was supplying Eden with what the people of the Forgotten desperately needed. People like Faye. That made Jac resent him. However, he needed him, especially if he planned on getting into Eden.

"What about the people here?" Jac asked.

"The people here aren't able to pay me what Eden pays me," he said, "An I have a family to look after, back in Ireland," he went on. "So as I said, tonight you can get into one of those crates and once it's on the supply train, it'll take you to Eden. Once you're in Eden, that's my part done. Staying in Eden without getting caught or killed is on you," Hugh said.

"How do you get the crates onto the supply train?" Jac questioned.

"Oh, I forgot to mention, the Blues will be here to load up the crates. They put them onto a big truck and drive them to a supply station on the Welsh border," Hugh said. Jac knew of this supply station but wasn't happy to hear mention of the Blues. Not only was Hugh supplying Eden but he was also getting assistance from the Blues. That explained how Little Dublin had remained untouched. Jac simply nodded. "Well, good luck to ye, you'll need it," Hugh laughed, nudging him. Once nightfall was upon them, as arranged, Jac climbed into an empty crate. The Blues arrived at the warehouse and Hugh's men assisted them with loading the crates onto a big truck of theirs. Once loaded, the Blues departed from Little Dublin and arrived at the Welsh border. From there, the crates were loaded onto the supply train. Hugh was right, no one checked them. They must have really trusted Hugh O'Shea, which made Jac wonder, how long had he been supplying Eden?

The supply train left the Welsh border. As Jac sat quietly in the crate, he thought about how he would avoid being killed on arrival. He'd need to be quick, that much was certain. He knew there was no turning back now. He had lied to his friends and told them he was going to Ireland. He had handed all of his bits to Hugh and he was now hiding in a crate, onboard a train heading to Eden. He took out the Cortexes and the little white light lit up the inside of the crate.

"I'll see you again soon," he whispered to it, as though Faye herself could hear him.

Chapter Seven
Welcome To Eden

The supply train came to a gradual stop. Jac had remained focused and ready the whole way there. He heard what he perceived to be a faint beeping alarm and doors closing. He figured it was the supply train's entrance into Eden. The crate was padded and cancelled out most of the noise. After approximately twenty minutes, they began to unload the crates from the train. Soon, he felt himself moving and then he stopped again. There was a thud, meaning that the crate he was in had been placed down. After a moment, he very carefully peeked out. It took him a moment for his eyes to adjust to the brightness. The inside of the crate was mostly dark and here, there were bright lights everywhere. It seemed that the crate he was in had been placed amongst all the others. He could see Whites as well as workers entering the supply train. He was definitely in Eden. He glanced around. There was no one near him so he quickly leapt out of the crate and hid behind it. No one had seen him. He noticed there were surveillance cameras on the ceiling but thankfully, none were facing him. He looked around for a way out and his eyes fell upon a door to his right that had 'Exit' written on it. Just what Jac needed. He made sure, once again, that no one was looking. Once he was confident, he sprinted towards the door and pushed it open. He hurried down a corridor and pushed through another door into another corridor and into another, somehow without seeing anyone. Finally, he went through one door and came out into a lobby area. There was a desk with a smartly dressed woman sat at it, preoccupied by a man attempting to charm her, who was wearing white overalls.

Two more men dressed the same passed through the lobby and went through a door to Jac's left. There was a pleasant poster on the wall of a beautiful, green forest that Jac found himself drawn to.

"Seeing you is the best part about working here," The man stood at the desk said, to which the woman blushed.

"You're so sweet," she squeaked. Somehow Jac needed to get past them and out of the front door. More men in white overalls came and went. Jac needed a distraction.

There were also surveillance cameras in the lobby but if Jac remained undetected, the cameras were of no concern.

"Hey Ellis, come on," a man called, emerging from a doorway.

"I got to go, but I'll be back soon," the man winked.

"I'll be waiting," the woman said back. Once lover boy had left, only the woman at the desk remained but still, Jac needed to get by. To Jac's delight, the woman swiveled in her chair and began rummaging through a drawer behind her.

Without hesitation, Jac hurried across the lobby and burst through the main doors. The woman turned around just as the lobby doors closed behind him. As Jac exited the building, he stopped immediately and looked up. He couldn't believe his eyes. Above him was a beautiful blue sky.

"Wow," he mumbled to himself. He stood there for a moment, staring.

"Is everything alright?" a voice asked, claiming Jac's attention. He looked straight ahead to see a man wearing the same white overalls.

"Uh, uh yeah," Jac said. The man looked Jac up and down, from his equally blue eyes to his grubby black boots. Jac wondered what the man was looking at and then he realized, he stood out. As Jac glanced around, almost everyone was wearing clothes of lighter colors - pale blues, whites and such.

There was Jac, wearing all black. Without saying anything else, Jac moved past the man and continued on. 'I need to find Avalon' he thought to himself. Due to his apparel, he was concerned that he would attract more unwanted attention but he didn't have a change of clothes and he was so bewildered that he walked on through the big, open streets.

For the first time, Jac felt as though he could properly breath. He was in awe. Eden was better than he had ever imagined. Everyone looked healthy and happy. There were huge buildings and tall trees lining the neatly placed pavements. There were e-cars that moved silently, and Jac was almost hit by one as he was crossing a road because he didn't hear it coming. It smelt fresh, a smell that Jac couldn't recall. There were no homeless people or beggars, no litter, no graffiti, and everything was clean. It was almost impossible for Jac to stay focused on finding Avalon but he felt the Cortexes in his pocket and it reminded him. The happy faces of the people turned to looks of displeasure as Jac passed them. More and more people were becoming aware of his abnormal presence. Walking through the streets of Eden didn't help him stay inconspicuous. It wasn't long before the Whites had seen him and were approaching him from across the street. Jac quickly turned a corner, narrowly missing a woman pushing a baby in a pram.

"My bad," he apologized. He hurried along and came to a huge domed building with a digital sign at the entrance reading "Apex Mall." He glanced over his shoulder to see that the Whites were still pursuing him. He entered the mall, hoping to lose them. There was a mall in the Forgotten but it was nothing like this one. There were a variety of different shops and shoppers, each holding shopping bags. Jac hoped that he would be able to lose the Whites in the mall but regardless, he still stood out. Besides, everyone distanced themselves from him. The Whites that were pursuing him also entered the mall, and soon there were more Whites coming from the other direction. The intense presence of them, armed, made the people disperse, leaving Jac in a big open space.

"Do not move!" One of them shouted, aiming an assault rifle at him. The people formed a circle around him and the Whites, watching. Clearly wearing all black wasn't something that people did in Eden. There was no where Jac could go. He reluctantly raised his hands.

"Okay," Jac huffed. He didn't know how he would get himself out of this one. Once the Whites surrounded him, one of them patted him down, feeling the Cortexes. The White attempted to reach into his inner pocket to get them but Jac grabbed his arm. "That's mine," he scowled. Another White grabbed Jac's shoulder, and Jac responded by elbowing him in his helmet.

The man grunted and the onlookers gasped. At that moment, he was whacked across the head with an assault rifle, cutting him. He dropped to his knees, blood dripped upon the clean white floor of the mall. The White snatched the Cortexes out of Jac's pocket and was surprised by what he found. "I said that's mine!" Jac raged, taking the White to the ground and unleashing a flurry of punches. Then, with a thud, everything went black.

As Jac came around, he was being lifted out of a vehicle, a White holding each of his arms and his hands cuffed. They carried him towards a building with big letters saying EDP above the main door. The Whites took him through the building to a room where they sat him in a chair. They uncuffed him and fastened his hands to the chair with metal clasps and stood. Soon after, a woman, with blonde hair in a ponytail came in. She was wearing a white suit with a white shirt. She had a stern, snotty look on her face.

"What's your name?" she asked him, standing opposite him. He ignored her. "Your name?" she insisted, she seemed impatient. Still, Jac said nothing. With a slight head nod from her, a White punched Jac in the face. "Name," she said.

"Jac," he said bluntly.

"My name's Chloe," she introduced, her demeanor altering. "You're from the Forgotten," she said, again he said nothing. "I can smell the filth on you," she uttered, unamused by his lack of response. "You had this...," she said, holding up the Cortexes. "These have been modified, and this one contains someone's consciousness." Jac stared at her. "Who's consciousness is this?" She asked him. "A lover?" she taunted. Yet again, he remained silent. The White punched him in the stomach. Jac groaned and spluttered.

She put the Cortexes away and leaned in.

"How did you get into Eden?" She questioned, staring him in the eyes. Silence. Again, a White punched him. "How did scum like you get into Eden?" she kept on.

"The front door," Jac muttered, smirking slightly. She leaned back and once again, the White punched him. Jac spat blood, almost onto the White's boots. Chloe was really becoming impatient with him.

"How did you get into Eden?" she asked again, more aggressively. Nothing, followed by another punch. Chloe stared down at him. "Fine, I'll have this deconstructed, and whoever's consciousness it contains, shall be lost," she stated. "I'll be back shortly," she told the Whites standing by.

Jac's facial expression changed to a look of anger. This pleased Chloe. She turned and left.

"Fucking bitch!" Jac shouted. He received a final punch, blood splattering as a result. Jac needed to get those Cortexes before Chloe deconstructed them. He immediately thought of something that Maddox had told him about when he had been arrested by the Blues. 'If they need you for information, the worst thing that can happen for them is you dying,' he had said. Jac teased one of the Whites. "You hit like a little girl," he laughed. The White, submitting to his ego, retaliated and punched Jac again, and this time Jac reacted differently. He pretended to choke. At first, the Whites ignored him and were even pleased with it but as he continued, they became concerned.

"What's happening to him?" One of them asked.

"I don't know, he's choking," the other replied. They shook him and moved his head down but still he continued to choke. It was very convincing.

As he had hoped, one of them unfastened the metal clasps and was about to pull him from the chair when suddenly he stopped. He front kicked the White in the head, knocking him out immediately. He then stood and right hooked the other one, stunning him. Jac then grabbed the White by his armor and rammed him, head first, into the chair, knocking him unconscious too. Jac took one of their assault rifles and a handgun before hurrying after Chloe, a look of fury in his blue eyes.

Chapter Eight
The Gateway

As Jac marched down a corridor in the direction he had seen Chloe go, his head rapidly moved left to right, glancing into different rooms, searching for her. He almost walked right into a man carrying a stack of papers, wearing a white shirt with a badge reading 'EDP' and 'George' beneath it. The man was startled by Jac's presence.

"Excu-"

Wasting no time, Jac whacked the man across the head with the rifle and continued on. The papers erupted like confetti, littering the floor as the man collapsed. After walking down another corridor, he finally came to a room that somewhat resembled a lab.

Chloe was there, accompanied by three Whites and two men wearing white overcoats, who had their backs to the door. As Jac burst in, everyone spun around. Jac spotted the Cortexes in Chloe's hand. There was a look of sheer worry on her face. It was mere seconds before guns were blazing and bullets whizzed in all directions. As windows shattered, small pieces of glass danced across the floor. While attempting to flee, one of the men wearing a white overcoat was caught in the crossfire and gunned down, his white overcoat becoming smeared with blood. Chloe and the other man took cover behind a desk as Jac remained in the doorway, squeezing the trigger of the assault rifle. One by one, the three Whites dropped. Then the gunfire stopped. Only Chloe and one remaining white coat stood between him and the Cortexes. Click, click. The assault rifle was out of ammo, so Jac threw it down and took out the handgun.

"Give me the Cortexes!" he demanded, moving towards her. Chloe panted. Suddenly an alarm began ringing out throughout the whole building. It wouldn't be long before Jac would be outnumbered. The white coat beside Chloe darted out from behind the desk towards a door. With one pull of the trigger, the man fell to the floor with a bullet hole in his back. Chloe gasped. She suddenly realized the severity of the situation she was in. She had mistaken Jac for some ordinary reprobate from the Forgotten, unaware that he had such experience with firearms. Jac's father had taught him how to shoot after he had returned from the war.

"Okay!" she whimpered aloud. Jac stopped, handgun ready. Chloe slowly emerged from behind the desk, hands raised, the Cortexes held in one of them.

"Pass them to me," he ordered, with one hand outstretched. She complied and handed them to him, Jac was glad to see that the glowing white light was still there. As Jac took the Cortexes, Chloe pulled out a handgun of her own. She wasn't quick enough though. Jac unloaded two rounds into Chloe's chest. With a grunt, she fell backwards, landing on the floor. The glass crunched beneath her. Jac returned the Cortexes to his inner pocket and tucked the handgun into his belt. He then took another assault rifle from one of the dead EDP and hurried out of the room. Jac wasn't sure how to leave the building. He ran blindly down corridors, the alarm ringing in his ears. At the end of one corridor, Jac saw a few EDP but they didn't see him. Luckily for him, he then found a backdoor leading into a car park where a few EDP vehicles were charging. He didn't know the first thing about driving an electric vehicle so he went on foot, moving between the vehicles as cover. No one seemed to be pursuing him. Once he was a comfortable distance from the EDP station, he stopped and gathered his breath, composing himself once again. After that, the EDP would be looking all over Eden for him so he needed to find Avalon and fast.

He attempted to conceal the assault rifle in his long, leather overcoat as he walked. He was intent on avoiding as many people as possible this time, something he should have done at the beginning, had he not been distracted by Eden itself. The sound of the alarm from the EDP station faded the further away he got. The same thought pinballed through his mind – 'I need to find Avalon.'

As he walked hopelessly through the backstreets of Eden, EDP Vehicles with their sirens blaring were patrolling the streets in search of him. There were also drones flying overhead. He noticed men on foot too, and he overheard them asking people if they had seen him. So far, no one had. But he was beginning to lose hope of finding Avalon before they would find him.

He sat down in a doorway, in an alley. It was well shadowed by the taller, surrounding buildings. His black clothing helped him blend in. To his left, he could see into the street, with people and cars occasionally passing by. There was also a huge screen on the side of a building playing advertisements.

'Hello, I'm Jonathan Eden, the founding father of Eden,' a voice on the screen said. Jac turned his head to look. 'Do you want to live after death? Well, you can ensure that you will. Get your Cortex now and secure your place in Avalon. For more information, go to the Gateway.' Jac's eyes widened. He now had a face to put to the name of Jonathan Eden. Jonathan looked like a smart, clean shaven, well-groomed man with a head of greyish-brown hair. He had some sort of white device attached to his head, covering his ears. Jac leapt to his feet and continued watching the screen. The screen then showed a big building with huge, elaborate doors. That place had to be the Gateway that Jonathan Eden mentioned. Jac needed to get somewhere higher up so that he could get a good view of Eden.

He continued on through the alleys, looking for a way to climb onto a rooftop. He was glad there was no one dwelling in the alleys like there would have been in the Forgotten. He thought about climbing onto some bins and then onto the roof of a smaller building and from there jumping to a higher building but the gap was too wide. He didn't want to risk breaking his legs, not now. But thankfully for him, he stumbled upon a ladder leading up to a roof. Once he was certain there were no drones flying overhead, he climbed it. It wasn't a very tall building but it was tall enough to get a good view. Once up, he crouched towards the edge and peered down into the busy street where more EDP vehicles were. He squinted his eyes and surveyed the distance. There, not too far away, was the building he had seen on the screen, the building he presumed to be the Gateway. Its big doors were visible from here. As more drones were approaching, he quickly hurried back towards the ladder and descended.

The problem was, he'd need to go to the other side of the street, somehow, without being seen. He returned to the same doorway and watched as the EDP vehicles drove away. He looked up and the sky seemed clear, and the drones had passed. He knew that anyone passing by would see him but as long as it wasn't the Whites, he was good. He took a deep breath. Once ready, he hauled himself out of the shadows and across the road, avoiding a passing car and into another alleyway.

"Hey you!" someone had shouted. Jac didn't look back. He continued running. He turned right and then left. He then heard someone shouting, 'He went down there!' They were clearly alerting the EDP of his whereabouts. He couldn't stop now.

He ran out, once again, into the street, startling more people. This time, there were no other alleyways, so he had to carry on down the main street. The pedestrians parted as he came bundling through. It wasn't long before a drone was following him overhead and EDP vehicles were doing so on the road. He ran as fast as he could, assault rifle in hand, towards the Gateway. As he came to the steps of the Gateway, Jac took cover behind a small wall. Two EDP vehicles pulled up in front of him as Whites jumped out. Jac opened fire.

The bullets ricocheted off of the armored exterior of the vehicles as the Whites took cover behind, firing back. The wall Jac was hiding behind was crumbling. He needed to get up the steps and inside. He reloaded his assault rifle and as he opened fire again, he ran. He made his way up the steps, still firing as he did so. The Whites continued to shoot back. As he got to the big front doors and pushed one open, a bullet ripped through his lower leg. He yelled out in agony and dived inside, dropping his assault rifle at the entrance.

As he laid on the floor, looking up, the Whites were still shooting and bullets were hitting the door. Above him, Jac noticed that the entrance had security doors. He scrambled to his feet and limped to the front desk where a woman was cowering behind it.

"Please don't shoot me!" she pleaded as Jac stood, untucking his handgun. "Close the security doors! Now!" He shouted. The lady pressed a small button hidden beneath the desk and the security doors slid down, blocking out the outside light. All went quiet. More EDP vehicles arrived at the building, as Whites surrounded it.

"Where is Avalon?" he asked her. With trembling hands, she pointed to a hallway to Jac's left.

"Come with me," he said. She looked up at him, eyes watering.

"Please," she begged.

"Come on, move it!" he beckoned. She reluctantly stood and walked around the desk to him. He assessed the bullet wound in his leg by prodding it. He groaned, his fingertips were red. "Take me there, take me to Avalon," he demanded.

With blood trickling, he limped behind her, further into the building. He was surprised that there were no guards inside the building. He assumed that it was probably because nothing like this had ever happened in Eden before. There were no employees there either, they must have fled or were hiding. He could hear the drones buzzing around outside like giant wasps, circling the building. With his finger on the trigger, he followed her. They came to a big, open room and there before him was Avalon, like he had seen on Rhys's computer back at the Den, only more impressive in person. Jac felt relieved.

"Go, go on," he said, shoeing her away with his gun. The lady scurried, her heels clacking as she went.

It was a magnificent machine of white and gold, emitting a white glow. The only sound was Jac's limping footsteps upon the marble floor as he slowly approached it. That was it, that was what he had come for. He could now finally reunite with Faye.

Chapter Nine

Hello Faye

As Jac moved closer, a voice spoke out.

"You must be the outsider," it said. Jac looked around and there, appearing from behind a pillar beside Avalon, was Jonathan Eden himself. He was wearing a crisp, white, three piece suit and white shirt with an equally white tie fastened around his neck. Jac aimed his handgun.

"Don't move," Jac said. Jonathan ignored him and did anyway.

"I heard you have a Cortex," Jonathan stated as he walked, calmly, around Jac, noticing his wounded leg.

"How did you know?" Jac asked.

"My daughter told me that an outsider had entered Eden and was carrying a Cortex," he told him. 'Daughter?' Jac thought to himself. Could that have been Chloe? "Who's consciousness does it contain? May I ask?" he said, rather politely. Jac saw no need to lie.

"My wife's," he confessed, keeping his gun aimed.

"I see," Jonathan sighed. "Do you know why I built Avalon?"

"No," Jac responded.

"My wife was killed by some lowlife degenerate from the Forgotten. Neither me nor my daughter got to say goodbye," Jonathan explained, moving closer. "I built this," he pointed to the peculiar white device, concealing his ears. "It's linked to my brain, accessing my memories. It allows me to see my wife as though she is right there in front of me but of course, she isn't."

Jac said nothing. "Then I built Avalon so then the people of Eden may be reunited with their loved ones upon death in a beautifully constructed virtual heaven. Unlike me, they will see their real husbands and wives, thanks to the Cortex," he continued, moving closer still. "I have built many wonderful things here in Eden. The blue sky over Eden is visible because of A.A.P, an advanced atmosphere purifier," He said proudly. "Another invention of mine, it keeps the smog away." There was a brief silence "I admire your determination to come to Eden with a Cortex containing your wife's consciousness but it was people like you, people from the Forgotten, that killed my wife… as you killed my daughter," he said, his fists clenching. That confirmed Jac's suspicion that Chloe was indeed Chloe Eden, daughter of Jonathan Eden.

"She took the Cortexes from me," Jac scowled, steadying his aim as Jonathan's blank facial expression turned to one of hatred and malice.

"The only remaining thing I had left in this world and you took it from me, you good-for-nothing, filthy outsider!" he spat, stepping forward. Jac was about to pull the trigger when Jonathan reached out, grabbed his arm tightly with a synthetic hand and crushed it. Jac howled, dropping the handgun. With his other hand, Jonathan grabbed Jac by the throat, lifted him and threw him at a pillar.

The pillar crumbled on impact. Jac landed, winded, gasping for breath. He was unprepared for Jonathan's strength. He must have been wearing an exoskeleton. Jonathan picked up the handgun and opened fire. Jac hurled himself behind the pillar as bullets hit it, sending chunks of marble flying. The sound of the gunfire echoed, disrupting the calmness of the room. The handgun then clicked, signifying that it was now out of bullets. Jonathan tossed it away.

"Come out!" he shouted. Jac came from behind the pillar, his back aching. He staggered towards Jonathan, fists clenched. The two of them exchanged blows. With the help of the exoskeleton, Jonathan hit harder. Soon, Jac's face was bloodied. Jonathan then kicked Jac right in the wound on his leg. He folded to the floor, grunting in pain.

"Look at you, you and all the rest from the Forgotten," he said, standing over him. "There's a reason it's called the Forgotten, just as you will be forgotten," he taunted before grabbing Jac by his collar and lifting him up. The two of them were face to face. Jac's leg was bleeding profusely, his face had been pummeled, and he could taste the blood in his mouth. Jac heard what sounded like the security door opening and approaching footsteps.

"Now I shall hand you over to the EDP," he smiled.

In one last attempt, Jac swung his fist and punched the left side of Jonathan Eden's headpiece, denting it and breaking his own hand in the process. Jonathan yelped in agony, letting go of Jac who fell to the ground once more. Jonathan Eden stepped back, disorientated, his head spasming. With all of his remaining strength, Jac got up and moved towards Avalon, dragging his leg behind him.

Finally he reached it. He took out the Cortexes, plugged them into Avalon and grabbed the black cable. Whites poured into the room as Jonathan collapsed. "There he is!" one of the Whites shouted as Jac held the cable to the top of his head, closed his eyes and...

For a moment, all there was, was blinding white, and then things began to come into focus. He could see thick brown trees topped with an assemblage of green leaves, and above that was a beautiful, deep blue sky. Beneath his feet was soft grass and tree roots, protruding from the earth's surface. There, stood before him, was the most beautiful thing of all - Faye. "Hello Faye," he said.

Faye looked at him with both happiness and bewilderment.

"Jac," she said back. An enormous smile appeared on his now unscathed face.

"Hello," He said again. She hurried towards him and he opened his arms wide and embraced her, the familiar smell of her perfume filling the air.

"Is this a dream?" she asked, pulling away from him, her eyes full of tears.

"No sweet, this is real," he beamed, as the two of them kissed, a sensation he had longed for.

"But how?" she wondered, looking around. "Where are we?" Their surroundings looked oddly familiar to Jac. It was indeed the poster he had seen in the lobby in Eden.

"I don't know," he smiled. It didn't matter to him. What mattered was that he and Faye were together.

Faye then remembered about the Cortex she had given him. She suddenly looked confused.

"Jac… did you store my consciousness?" she asked him, still holding him.

"I did," he confessed, still smiling. "When you died, part of me died too. I took your consciousness, as you said, and kept it with me everywhere I went but I just couldn't stand to live without you Faye… I couldn't," Jac declared. "I found out that a Cortex could be uploaded to a machine called Avalon and then that person would live on in a virtual heaven," He explained. "I found a way into Eden, where Avalon was, and I uploaded your consciousness, and mine."

"So, you're dead?" She asked sorrowfully. "No Faye, this is the most alive I've felt in a long time," he laughed. The happiness radiating from him brought a smile to Faye's face too.

"This place is beautiful," she said, letting go of him, taking it all in.

"It is," he agreed. Jac reached out a hand. "Walk with me," he said. Faye took his hand and held it tightly. Together, they walked, side by side through the forest, beneath the trees, through the beams of sunlight in quiet solitude.

The end?

Printed in Great Britain
by Amazon